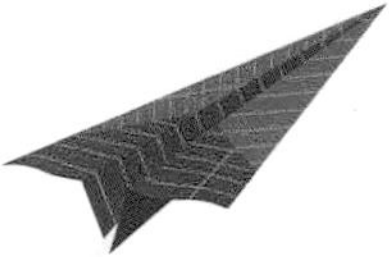

ROALD DAHL'S

INCREDIBLE INVENTIONS

working in partnership with National Literacy Trust

ILLUSTRATED BY QUENTIN BLAKE

PUFFIN

PUFFIN BOOKS

UK | USA | Canada | Ireland | Australia
India | New Zealand | South Africa

Puffin Books is part of the Penguin Random House group of companies
whose addresses can be found at global.penguinrandomhouse.com.

puffinbooks.com

Penguin
Random House
UK

Made for McDonald's 2015
001

Charlie and the Chocolate Factory: first published in the USA by Alfred A. Knopf, Inc., 1964,
and in Great Britain by George Allen & Unwin 1967
George's Marvellous Medicine: first published in Great Britain by Jonathan Cape 1981
Published in paperback by Puffin Books

Printed in Slovakia

A CIP catalogue record for this book is available from the British Library

ISBN: 978–0–141–36251–9

Batch nr.: 123975/16

FSC
MIX
FSC® C022120

Explore the extraordinary world of

ROALD DAHL

It is full of people who come up
with BRILLIANT INVENTIONS.

George teaches his grandma a **lesson** she will never forget with a **marvellous** potion. And Willy Wonka is the most **amazing**, the most **extraordinary** chocolate maker the world has **ever** seen! (We thought *everyone* knew that!)

Bring Roald Dahl's extraordinary stories to life with the **Happy Studio** app. Simply download the app to a phone or tablet and read the stories in this book aloud to experience the fun.

What would **you** **invent** if you owned a chocolate factory?

The Inventing Room and The Great Gum Machine

from

CHARLIE AND THE CHOCOLATE FACTORY

When Mr Wonka shouted 'Stop the boat!' the Oompa-Loompas jammed their oars into the river and backed water furiously.

The boat stopped.

The Oompa-Loompas guided the boat alongside the red door.

On the door it said, INVENTING ROOM – PRIVATE – KEEP OUT. Mr Wonka took a key from his pocket, leaned over the side of the boat, and put the key in the keyhole.

'*This* is the most important room in the entire factory!' he said. 'All my most secret new inventions are cooking and simmering in here! Old Fickelgruber would give his front teeth to be allowed inside just for three minutes! So would Prodnose and Slugworth and all the other rotten chocolate makers! But now, listen to me! I want no messing about when you go in! No touching, no meddling, and no tasting! Is that agreed?'

'Yes, yes!' the children cried. 'We won't touch a thing!'

'Up to now,' Mr Wonka said, 'nobody else, not even an Oompa-Loompa, has ever been allowed in here!' He opened the door and stepped out of the boat into the room. The four children and their parents all scrambled after him.

'Don't touch!' shouted Mr Wonka. 'And don't knock anything over!'

Charlie Bucket stared around the gigantic room in which he now found himself. The place was like a witch's kitchen! All about him black metal pots were boiling and bubbling on huge stoves, and kettles were hissing and pans were sizzling,

and strange iron machines were clanking and spluttering, and there were pipes running all over the ceiling and walls, and the whole place was filled with smoke and steam and delicious rich smells.

Mr Wonka himself had suddenly become even more excited than usual, and anyone could see that this was the room he loved best of all. He was hopping about among the saucepans and the machines like a child among his Christmas

presents, not knowing which thing to look at first. He lifted the lid from a huge pot and took a sniff; then he rushed over and dipped a finger into a barrel of sticky yellow stuff and had a taste; then he skipped across to one of the machines and turned half a dozen knobs this way and that; then he peered anxiously through the glass door of a gigantic oven, rubbing his hands and cackling with delight at what he saw inside. Then he ran over

to another machine, a small shiny affair that kept going *phut-phut-phut-phut-phut*, and every time it went *phut*, a large green marble dropped out of it into a basket on the floor. At least it looked like a marble.

'Everlasting Gobstoppers!' cried Mr Wonka proudly. 'They're completely new! I am inventing them for children who are given very little pocket money. You can put an Everlasting Gobstopper in your mouth and you can suck it and suck it and suck it and suck it and it

will *never* get any smaller!'

'It's like gum!' cried Violet Beauregarde.

'It is *not* like gum,' Mr Wonka said. 'Gum is for chewing, and if you tried chewing one of these Gobstoppers here you'd break your teeth off! And they *never* get any smaller! They *never* disappear! *NEVER!* At least I don't think they do. There's one of them being tested this very moment in the Testing Room next door. An Oompa-Loompa is sucking it. He's been sucking it for very nearly a year now without stopping, and it's still just as good as ever!

'Now, over here,' Mr Wonka went on, skipping excitedly across the room to the opposite wall, 'over here I am inventing a completely new line in toffees!' He stopped beside a large saucepan. The saucepan was full of a thick gooey purplish treacle, boiling and bubbling. By standing on his toes, little Charlie could just see inside it.

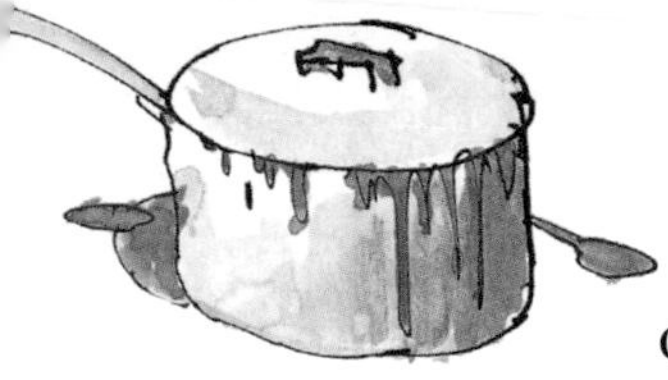

'That's Hair Toffee!' cried Mr Wonka. 'You eat just one tiny bit of that, and in exactly half an hour a brand-new luscious thick silky beautiful crop of hair will start growing out all over the top of your head! And a moustache! And a beard!'

'A beard!' cried Veruca Salt. 'Who wants a beard, for heaven's sake?'

'It would suit you very well,' said Mr Wonka, 'but unfortunately the mixture is not quite right yet. I've got it too strong.

It works too well. I tried it on an Oompa-Loompa yesterday in the Testing Room and immediately a huge black beard started shooting out of his chin, and the beard grew so fast that soon it was trailing all over the floor in a thick hairy carpet. It was growing faster than we could cut it! In the end we had to use a lawn mower to keep it in check! But I'll get the mixture right soon! And when I do, then there'll be no excuse any more for little boys and girls going about with bald heads!'

'But Mr Wonka,' said Mike Teavee, 'little boys and girls never *do* go about with . . .'

'Don't argue, my dear child, *please* don't argue!' cried Mr Wonka. 'It's such a waste of precious time! Now, over *here*, if you will all step this way, I will show you something that I am terrifically proud of. Oh, do be careful! Don't knock anything over! Stand back!'

Mr Wonka led the party over to a gigantic machine that stood in the very centre of the Inventing Room. It was a mountain of gleaming metal that towered high above the children and their parents.

Out of the very top of it there sprouted hundreds and hundreds of thin glass tubes, and the glass tubes all curled downwards and came together in a bunch and hung suspended over an enormous round tub as big as a bath.

'Here we go!' cried Mr Wonka, and he pressed three different buttons on the side of the machine. A second later, a mighty rumbling sound came from inside it, and the whole machine began to shake most frighteningly, and steam began hissing out of it all over, and then suddenly the watchers noticed that runny stuff was pouring down the insides of all the hundreds of little glass tubes and squirting out into the great tub below. And in every single tube the runny stuff was of a different colour, so that all the colours of the rainbow (and many others as well) came sloshing and splashing into the tub. It was a lovely sight. And when the tub was nearly

full, Mr Wonka pressed another button, and immediately the runny stuff disappeared, and a whizzing whirring noise took its place; and then a giant whizzer started whizzing round inside the enormous tub, mixing up all the different coloured liquids like an ice-cream soda. Gradually, the mixture began to froth. It became frothier and frothier, and it turned from blue to white to green to brown to yellow, then back to blue again.

'Watch!' said Mr Wonka.

Click went the machine, and the whizzer stopped whizzing. And now there came a sort of sucking noise, and very quickly all the blue frothy mixture in the huge basin was sucked back into the stomach of the machine. There was a moment of silence. Then a few queer rumblings were heard. Then silence again. Then suddenly, the machine let out a monstrous mighty groan, and at the same moment a tiny drawer (no bigger than the drawer in

a slot machine) popped out of the side of the machine, and in the drawer there lay something so small and thin and grey that everyone thought it must be a mistake. The thing looked like a little strip of grey cardboard.

The children and their parents stared at the little grey strip lying in the drawer.

'You mean that's *all*?' said Mike Teavee, disgusted.

'That's all,' answered Mr Wonka,

gazing proudly at the result. 'Don't you know what it is?'

There was a pause. Then suddenly, Violet Beauregarde, the silly gum-chewing girl, let out a yell of excitement. 'By gum, it's *gum*!' she shrieked. 'It's a stick of chewing-gum!'

'Right you are!' cried Mr Wonka, slapping Violet hard on the back. 'It's a stick of gum! It's a stick of the most *amazing* and *fabulous* and *sensational* gum in the world!'

Willy Wonka invents Everlasting Gobstoppers and Hair Toffee. What **extraordinary** sweets would **you** invent?

Draw your **sweets** here.

Do you have the **Happy Studio** app downloaded?
Launch it **now** for an **extra** activity!

I want to make a **terrific whopping exploding shocker** for Grandma!

George Begins to Make the Medicine

from

GEORGE'S MARVELLOUS MEDICINE

George took an enormous saucepan out of the cupboard and placed it on the kitchen table.

'George!' came the shrill voice from the next room. 'What are you doing?'

'Nothing, Grandma,' he called out.

'You needn't think I can't hear you just because you closed the door! You're rattling the saucepans!'

'I'm just tidying the kitchen, Grandma.'

Then there was silence.

George had absolutely no doubts whatsoever about how he was going to make his famous medicine. He wasn't going to fool about wondering whether to put in a little bit of this or a little bit of that. Quite simply, he was going to put in EVERYTHING he could find. There would be no messing about, no hesitating, no wondering whether a particular thing would knock the old girl sideways or not. The rule would be this: whatever he saw, if it was runny or powdery or gooey, in it went.

Nobody had ever made a medicine like that before. If it didn't actually cure Grandma, then it would anyway cause some exciting results. It would be worth watching.

George decided to work his way round the various rooms one at a time and see what they had to offer.

He would go first to the bathroom. There are always lots of funny things in a bathroom. So upstairs he went, carrying the enormous two-handled saucepan before him.

In the bathroom, he gazed longingly at the famous and dreaded medicine cupboard. But he didn't go near it. It was the only thing in the entire house he was forbidden to touch. He had made solemn promises to his parents about this and he wasn't going to break them. There were things in there, they had told him, that could actually kill a person, and although he was out to give Grandma a pretty fiery mouthful, he didn't really want a dead body on his hands. George put the saucepan on the floor and went to work.

Number one was a bottle labelled GOLDEN GLOSS HAIR SHAMPOO. He emptied it into the pan. 'That ought to wash her tummy nice and clean,' he said.

He took a full tube of TOOTHPASTE and squeezed out the whole lot of it in one long worm. 'Maybe that will brighten up those horrid brown teeth of hers,' he said.

There was an aerosol can of SUPERFOAM SHAVING SOAP belonging to his father. George loved playing with aerosols. He pressed the button and kept his finger on it until there was nothing left. A wonderful mountain of white foam built up in the giant saucepan.

With his fingers, he scooped out the contents of a jar of VITAMIN ENRICHED FACE CREAM.

In went a small bottle of scarlet NAIL VARNISH. 'If the toothpaste doesn't clean her teeth,' George said, 'then this will paint them as red as roses.'

He found another jar of creamy stuff labelled HAIR REMOVER. SMEAR IT ON YOUR LEGS, it said, AND ALLOW TO REMAIN FOR FIVE MINUTES. George tipped it all into the saucepan.

There was a bottle with yellow stuff inside it called DISHWORTH'S FAMOUS DANDRUFF CURE. In it went.

There was something called BRILLIDENT FOR CLEANING FALSE TEETH. It was a white powder. In that went, too.

He found another aerosol can, NEVERMORE PONKING DEODORANT SPRAY, GUARANTEED, it said, TO KEEP AWAY UNPLEASANT BODY SMELLS FOR A WHOLE DAY. 'She could use plenty of that,' George said as he sprayed the entire canful into the saucepan.

LIQUID PARAFFIN, the next one was called. It was a big bottle. He hadn't the faintest idea what it did to you, but he poured it in anyway.

That, he thought, looking around him, was about all from the bathroom.

On his mother's dressing-table in the bedroom, George found yet another lovely aerosol can. It was called HELGA'S HAIRSET. HOLD TWELVE INCHES AWAY FROM THE HAIR AND SPRAY LIGHTLY. He squirted the whole lot into the saucepan. He *did* enjoy squirting these aerosols.

There was a bottle of perfume called FLOWERS OF TURNIPS. It smelled of old cheese. In it went.

And in, too, went a large round box of POWDER. It was called PINK PLASTER. There was a powder-puff on top and he threw that in as well for luck.

He found a couple of LIPSTICKS. He pulled the greasy red things out of their little cases and added them to the mixture.

The bedroom had nothing more to offer, so George carried the enormous saucepan downstairs again and trotted into the laundry-room where the shelves were full of all kinds of household items.

The first one he took down was a large box of SUPERWHITE FOR AUTOMATIC WASHING-MACHINES. DIRT, it said, WILL DISAPPEAR LIKE MAGIC. George didn't know whether Grandma was automatic or not, but she was certainly a dirty old woman. 'So she'd better have it all,' he said, tipping in the whole boxful.

Then there was a big tin of WAXWELL FLOOR POLISH. IT REMOVES FILTH AND FOUL MESSES FROM YOUR FLOOR AND LEAVES EVERYTHING SHINY

BRIGHT, it said. George scooped the orange-coloured waxy stuff out of the tin and plonked it into the pan.

There was a round cardboard carton labelled FLEA POWDER FOR DOGS. KEEP WELL AWAY FROM THE DOG'S FOOD, it said, BECAUSE THIS POWDER, IF EATEN, WILL MAKE THE DOG EXPLODE. 'Good,' said George, pouring it all into the saucepan.

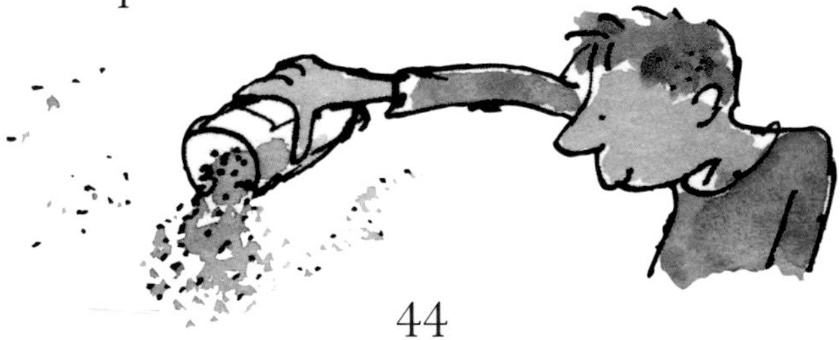

He found a box of CANARY SEED on the shelf. 'Perhaps it'll make the old bird sing,' he said, and in it went.

Next, George explored the box with shoe-cleaning materials – brushes and tins and dusters. 'Well now,' he thought, 'Grandma's medicine is brown, so *my* medicine must also be

brown or she'll smell a rat.' The way to colour it, he decided, would be with BROWN SHOE-POLISH. The large tin he chose was labelled DARK TAN. Splendid. He scooped it all out with an old spoon and plopped it into the pan. He would stir it up later.

On his way back to the kitchen, George saw a bottle of GIN standing on the sideboard. Grandma was very fond of gin. She was allowed to have a small nip of it every evening. Now he would give her a treat. He would pour in the whole bottle. He did.

Back in the kitchen, George put the huge saucepan on the table and went over to the cupboard that served as a larder. The shelves were bulging with bottles and jars of every sort. He chose the following and emptied them one by one into the saucepan:

A TIN OF CURRY POWDER

A TIN OF MUSTARD POWDER

A BOTTLE OF 'EXTRA HOT' CHILLI SAUCE

A TIN OF BLACK PEPPERCORNS

A BOTTLE OF HORSERADISH SAUCE

'There!' he said aloud. 'That should do it!'

'George!' came the screechy voice from the next room. 'Who are you talking to in there? What are you up to?'

'Nothing, Grandma, absolutely nothing,' he called back.

'Is it time for my medicine yet?'

'No, Grandma, not for about half an hour.'

'Well, just see you don't forget it.'

'I won't, Grandma,' George answered. 'I promise I won't.'

At this point, George suddenly had an extra good wheeze. Although the medicine cupboard in the house was forbidden ground, what about the medicines his father kept on the shelf in the shed next to the henhouse? The animal medicines?

What about *those*?

Nobody had ever told him he mustn't touch *them*.

'Let's face it,' George said to himself, 'hair-spray and shaving-cream and shoe-polish are all very well and they

will no doubt cause some splendid explosions inside the old geezer, but what the magic mixture now needs is a touch of the real stuff, real pills and real tonics, to give it punch and muscle.'

George picked up the heavy three-quarters full saucepan and carried it out of the back door. He crossed the farmyard and headed straight for the shed alongside the henhouse. He knew his father wouldn't be there. He was out haymaking in one of the meadows.

George entered the dusty old shed and put the saucepan on the bench. Then he looked up at the medicine shelf. There were five big bottles there. Two were full of pills, two were full of runny stuff and one was full of powder.

‘I’ll use them all,’ George said. ‘Grandma needs them. Boy, does she need them!’

The first bottle he took down contained an orange-coloured powder. The label said, FOR CHICKENS WITH FOUL PEST, HEN GRIPE, SORE BEAKS, GAMMY LEGS, COCKERELITIS, EGG TROUBLE, BROODINESS OR LOSS OF FEATHERS. MIX ONE SPOONFUL ONLY WITH EACH BUCKET OF FEED.

'Well,' George said aloud to himself as he tipped in the whole bottleful, 'the old bird won't be losing any feathers after she's had a dose of this.'

The next bottle he took down had about five hundred gigantic purple pills in it. FOR HORSES WITH HOARSE THROATS, it said on the label. THE HOARSE-THROATED HORSE SHOULD SUCK ONE PILL TWICE A DAY.

'Grandma may not have a hoarse throat,' George said, 'but she's certainly got a sharp tongue. Maybe they'll cure that instead.' Into the saucepan went the five hundred gigantic purple pills.

Then there was a bottle of thick yellowish liquid. FOR COWS, BULLS AND BULLOCKS, the label said. WILL CURE COW POX, COW MANGE, CRUMPLED HORNS, BAD BREATH IN BULLS, EARACHE, TOOTHACHE, HEADACHE, HOOFACHE, TAILACHE AND SORE UDDERS.

'That grumpy old cow in the living-room has every one of those rotten illnesses,' George said. 'She'll need it all.' With a slop and a gurgle, the yellow liquid splashed into the now nearly full saucepan.

The next bottle contained a brilliant red liquid. SHEEPDIP, it said on the label. FOR SHEEP WITH SHEEPROT AND FOR GETTING RID OF TICKS AND FLEAS. MIX ONE SPOONFUL IN ONE GALLON OF WATER AND SLOSH IT OVER THE SHEEP. CAUTION, DO NOT MAKE THE MIXTURE ANY STRONGER OR THE WOOL WILL FALL OUT AND THE ANIMAL WILL BE NAKED.

'By gum,' said George, 'how I'd love

to walk in and slosh it all over old Grandma and watch the ticks and fleas go jumping off her. But I can't. I mustn't. So she'll have to drink it instead.' He poured the bright red medicine into the saucepan.

The last bottle on the shelf was full of pale green pills. PIG PILLS, the label announced. FOR PIGS WITH PORK PRICKLES, TENDER TROTTERS, BRISTLE BLIGHT AND SWINE SICKNESS. GIVE ONE PILL PER DAY. IN SEVERE CASES TWO PILLS MAY BE GIVEN, BUT MORE THAN

THAT WILL MAKE THE PIG ROCK AND ROLL.

'Just the stuff,' said George, 'for that miserable old pig back there in the house. She'll need a very big dose.' He tipped all the green pills, hundreds and hundreds of them, into the saucepan.

There was an old stick lying on the bench that had been used for stirring paint. George picked it up and started to stir his marvellous concoction. The mixture was as thick as cream, and as he stirred and stirred, many wonderful colours rose up from the depths and blended together, pinks, blues, greens, yellows and browns.

George went on stirring until it was all well mixed, but even so there were still hundreds of pills lying on the bottom that hadn't melted. And there was his mother's splendid powder-puff floating on the surface. 'I shall have to boil it all up,' George said. 'One good quick boil on the stove is all it needs.' And with that he staggered back towards the house with the enormous heavy saucepan.

On the way, he passed the garage, so he went in to see if he could find any other interesting things. He added the following:

Half a pint of ENGINE OIL – to keep Grandma's engine going smoothly.

Some ANTI-FREEZE – to keep her radiator from freezing up in winter.

A handful of GREASE – to grease her creaking joints.

Then back to the kitchen.

If you invented your own **marvellously disgusterous** mixture, which items from this list would you use?

A dollop of mud

Brussels sprouts

Crocodile eggs

Cod liver oil

Cabbage

Toenails

Vinegar

Cinnamon

Peacock feather

Pondweed

Horse hair

Stinky cheese

Pickled eggs

DO NOT give medicines to your ghastly grandma (or anyone else) – not all medicines are as marvellous as George's!

Can you think of a special name for your invention?

Do you have the **Happy Studio** app downloaded? Launch it **now** for an **extra** activity!